To Franny and Bou, the queens of my zoo.
— E.S.P.

For Tzvia, truly one in a million.
— J.U.

Text copyright © 2013 by Erica S. Perl
Illustrations copyright © 2013 by Jackie Urbanovic

Library of Congress Cataloging-in-Publication Data
Perl, Erica S.   •   King of the zoo / by Erica S. Perl ; illustrated by Jackie Urbanovic. — 1st ed.   •   p. cm.
Summary: Each of the animals at the zoo thinks of himself as King of the Zoo but Carlos the Chameleon is sure that the crown is his, and he has at least one ally.   •   ISBN 978-0-545-46182-5 (alk. paper)   •   1. Chameleons—Juvenile fiction.
2. Zoo animals—Juvenile fiction. [1. Chameleons—Fiction. 2. Lizards—Fiction. 3. Zoo animals—Fiction. 4. Animals—Fiction.]
I. Urbanovic, Jackie, ill. II. Title.   •   PZ7.P3163Kin 2013   •   813.6—dc23   •   2012035235

10 9 8 7 6 5 4 3 2 1   13 14 15 16 17

Printed in the U.S.A.   08   •   First edition, August 2013

The text was set in Chowderhead.   •   The art was created using watercolor and pencil.
Book design by Chelsea C. Donaldson

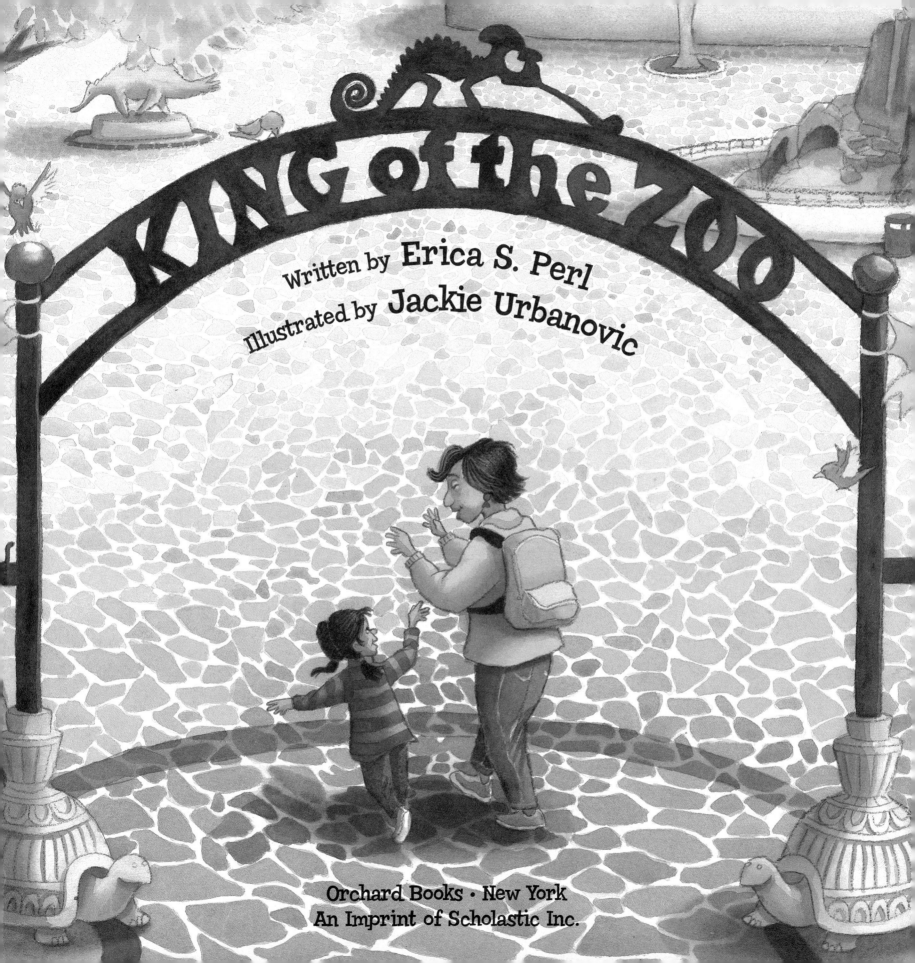

KING of the Zoo

Written by Erica S. Perl

Illustrated by Jackie Urbanovic

Orchard Books · New York
An Imprint of Scholastic Inc.

They say the lion is king of the jungle.

But who's king of the zoo?

5 TIGER

6 GIRAFFE

8 PYGMY SHREW

1 HIPPO

There was no one cooler or cleverer
or charming-er than Carlos.

Or so he thought.

Carlos was

hopping mad.

And then things
got even worse.
Carlos stomped his foot
in frustration.

And then things got
even worse.
Carlos stretched his neck
out stubbornly.

This had to stop.
There was only room for ONE king.

And that king is **ME, that's who!**

Carlos paced, green with envy.

Why did there have to be other kings of the zoo?

Carlos saw red.

It just wasn't fair!

He was the best king!

Carlos basked in a purple glow.

But **purple** gave way to **blue**.

Was he *still* the best king?

Or had he gotten a little **rusty**?

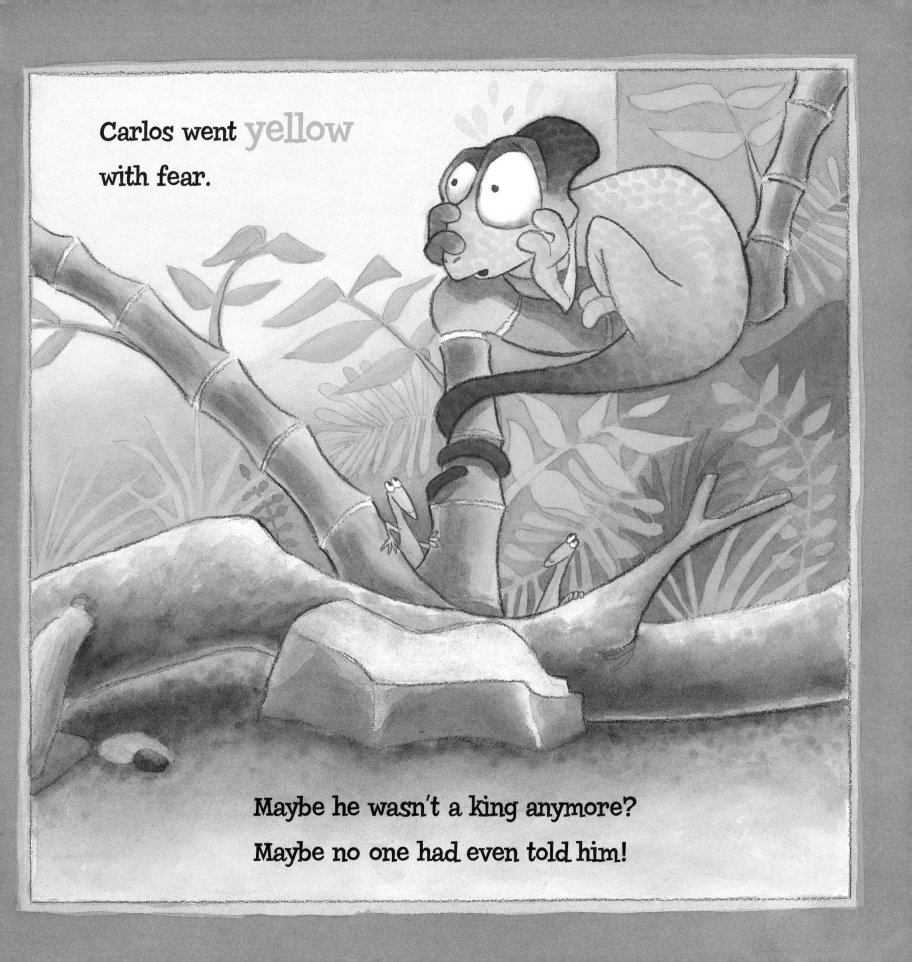

Carlos went yellow with fear.

Maybe he wasn't a king anymore?
Maybe no one had even told him!

Carlos blushed.

Somebody knew he ruled!

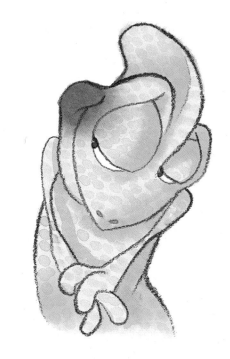

Just one single, solitary person.

But the funny thing was, it felt
like an entire kingdom.

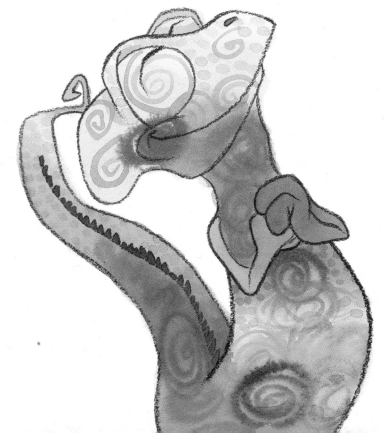